This one is for George, with love
Bernette Ford

For Archie and Dylan
love from Sam Williams

First published in Great Britain in 2008
by Boxer Books Limited
www.boxerbooks.com

This paperback edition published in 2008

ISBN 13: 978-1-905417-91-9

1 3 5 7 9 10 8 6 4 2

Printed in China

All of our papers are sourced from managed forests and renewable resources.

No More Dummy for Piggy!

Bernette Ford and Sam Williams

Boxer Books

Piggy knocks on Ducky's door.

He is sucking on his dummy.

Ducky peeks out the window.

"Peek-a-boo, Piggy!" she says.

"Do you want to play

a new game with me?"

Piggy nods his head up and down.

He tries to smile at Ducky,

but his dummy is in the way.

Ducky and Piggy run out to the garden.

Piggy giggles . . .

and drops his dummy on the ground.

"You can't have that now,"

says Ducky, "it's dirty!"

Piggy has another dummy

in his pocket.

He pops it into his mouth.

Now Ducky hides behind her hands.

"Peek-a-boo, Piggy!" Ducky shouts.

"Peek-a-boo! I see you!"

Piggy tries to smile at Ducky.

But his dummy is in the way.

Ducky hides behind a tree.

She peeks around it.

"Peek-a-boo, Piggy," calls Ducky.

"Peek-a-boo, I see you!"

Piggy laughs . . .

and drops his dummy on the ground!

He looks in his pocket for another.

But he doesn't have one.

Piggy starts to cry.

He points to his dummy in the dirt.

"What's the matter, Piggy?" asks Ducky.

"Don't you want to play with me?"

Piggy nods his head up and down.

Ducky picks up Piggy's dummy

and puts it on the table.

"You're missing all the fun," she says.

"Come on, it's your turn now!"

So Piggy hides behind a lawn chair.

"Peek-a-boo, Ducky!" Piggy says softly.

"Peek-a-boo, I see you!"

Ducky laughs!

Piggy hides under the table.

"Peek-a-boo, Ducky!" he calls louder.

"Peek-a-boo, I see you!"

Ducky laughs again.

The two friends play together for hours and Piggy forgets all about his dummy.

"Did you have fun today?" asks Ducky.

"Yes, I did!" Piggy shouts.

"No more dummy for Piggy!"

Other Boxer Books paperbacks

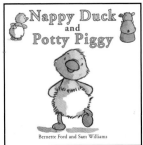

Nappy Duck and Potty Piggy: Bernette Ford & Sam Williams

A witty and subtle nappy-to-potty story, in which little ones help each other learn and grow. Perfect for reading together.

ISBN: 978-1-905417-00-1

No More Bottles for Bunny!: Bernette Ford & Sam Williams

An entertaining and gentle story that encourages children to start drinking from a cup.

ISBN: 978-1-905417-30-8

Tip Tip Dig Dig: Emma Garcia

A bright and inventive story for young children. Each construction vehicle does their own job as they all work together towards a surprise ending.

ISBN: 978-1-905417-84-1

Clip-Clop: Nicola Smee

Cat, Dog, Pig and Duck climb aboard Mr Horse for a ride and want to go faster and faster... but will faster lead to disaster?

ISBN: 978-1-905417-04-9